HAUNTED HOUSE BLUES

HAUNTED HOUSE BLUES

THERESA TOMLINSON

Illustrations by

GARETH FLOYD

WALKER BOOKS
AND SUBSIDIARIES

LONDON · BOSTON · SYDNEY

For Bluesman Sam

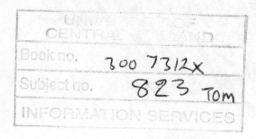

First published 1996 by Walker Books Ltd
87 Vauxhall Walk, London SE11 5HJ

2 4 6 8 10 9 7 5 3 1

Text © 1996 Theresa Tomlinson
Illustrations © 1996 Gareth Floyd

This book has been typeset in Plantin.

Printed in England

British Library Cataloguing in Publication Data
A catalogue record for this book
is available from the British Library.

ISBN 0-7445-4131-X

Contents

Walking in a Straight Line 7

A Lonely House 13

The Blues 21

The Holly and the Ivy 25

Mad Mason 33

Kind of ... Got Permission 41

Tilly's Tunes 47

Making Their Marks 53

The Attack 61

The Boy With the Pipe 65

Desperate Dan 73

Strange Visitors 79

The New Annexe 85

Banishing the Blues 89

Walking
in a Straight Line

Sally and I found the haunted house the day we decided to walk home from school in a straight line.

Our school, Holton Primary, stood in the far corner of a huge stretch of grounds. They were enormous grounds, almost like a park, with playing fields, tennis courts and a wood. There was even a bit of wilderness, with thick overgrown bushes, tall trees and stone steps that seemed to lead nowhere. We had to walk home through all of that, every day.

My parents fussed and nagged. "Danny!" they'd say. "You've to walk with Sally to and from school. You've to stay close together and come straight home!"

Sally was the girl who lived next door, and both our mothers worried like mad about us going near the woods. We thought they were daft. It wasn't the woods that frightened us. The only thing we were scared of was Gary Fox, his big friend Colin and the rest of their gang.

You see, right bang in the middle of this huge stretch of land was Holton Grange Comprehensive School, where all the secondary school kids went. Gary and his mates used to be at our school, but they'd moved on to the Comp. They were only a few years older than us, but they thought they were so grown up! They hung around at the edges of the woods, smoking and drinking and throwing cans about. They spoke in great loud voices, telling each other how much they hated younger kids like us. Sometimes they'd shout things at us. "Little Danny's got to walk home with a big girl!"

That got me really mad. Sally's not one of those wimpish girls, she's tough.

Sometimes they'd tease me by singing this soppy song.

Oh, Danny Boy ...
The pipes,
*   the pipes are calling...*

One time Colin snatched my duffle bag
and dumped it in a holly bush. He went red
in the face he was giggling so much. I had to
go scrabbling around in the bush to get it
back. Colin was big and stupid, but Gary Fox
was the one I hated most. He told Colin to
do it. I saw them whispering together as we
came along. Colin was daft enough to do
anything Gary told him.

Sally got really mad with them that day.
As soon as I got my bag back, she stuck her
tongue out at them and shouted, "Stupid
idiots!"

Then we both had to run for it!

Anyway, Sally and I made this plan – we
would walk straight home, just like our
mothers told us to. We'd walk in a dead
straight line, right through the middle of the
wilderness. Sally said she'd bring her

compass. We knew that if we walked due north we'd eventually come out somewhere on our street.

On the day that we tried the straight walk, we found the compass a great help. We walked north across the Comp playing field, along a path and over some neat clipped grass. Then we stopped and grinned at each other. If we wanted to keep on heading north we'd have to go straight for the wilderness, where thick laurel bushes and tall yew trees grew. It was just what we'd hoped would happen, so we took a deep breath and ploughed in. It wasn't easy going. We had to push away branches, and duck down in the thickest parts and wade through piles of dead leaves and prickly brambles.

"It's like that story," said Sally. "You know, where the prince goes hacking and chopping his way through the thorn bushes to get to the hidden palace. My hands are all scratched and my socks are getting ripped."

I looked up ahead through the branches

of the trees just then, and I couldn't believe my eyes. There in front of me was a high stone turret, with a round pointed roof and a small window.

"Sally," I whispered. "There's the palace."

Sally looked up, her eyes wide with astonishment.

We'd both completely forgotten about walking in a straight line.

A Lonely House

....

We went fast then, towards the house,
stamping on twigs and kicking at the
brambles. Then we slowed up as we got
really close. There were two grand carved
gateposts that were green with mould
and ivy, a huge boarded-up front entrance
with columns on either side and a flight
of steps strewn with litter and broken
glass.

Somehow neither of us wanted to speak.
What could we say? I could tell that Sally was
wildly excited by the way she whispered,
"Wow! Wow!"

The house was built of sandy-coloured
stone, very old and worn. We stared up at the
high dusty windows above the front door.
There were dark gaps on the roof where
slates were missing. Someone had written

rude words and funny signs on the boarded-up doorway. There were heaps of rubble and old drink cans all around. But still, despite the mess, bits of it were somehow wonderful. At the top of the house, right at the front, was a huge curved pattern, with diamond shapes cut into the stone. A carving of a fish curling round a sword was set right in the middle. Above it all was a beautiful fancy metalwork spike.

Right from the very start it made me feel sad. It was a brilliantly exciting thing to find, of course, better than anything we could have imagined, but still it made me terribly sad. I wanted to go and sit down on those rubbish-strewn steps and play a wailing tune on my mouth organ. A wailing, howling kind of tune that would drift up through the smashed stonework and windows, and echo under the broken roof slates.

Sally was staring down at the gravel filled with weeds beneath our feet.

"It's an old road," she said. "And it goes

round the corner."

"A road for the house," I said. "It's got its own private road ... or it had."

We followed the gravel driveway round the corner of the house, and even though it was covered in grass and weeds we could see where the broad old pathway used to curve down the hillside.

"Goes down from the house to the main road," said Sally.

"Down to the caretaker's cottage," I told her.

We wandered along the side of the house, peeping into windows and pulling away bits of ivy. We still didn't speak much, though I knew that we both had all sorts of ideas whizzing round in our heads.

Perhaps we could clean it up! We could use it as a den! Maybe it would have ghosts! It certainly looked as though it should.

"Shall we see what's round the back?" Sally whispered, but before I could answer, we heard something strange.

"What's that?" I hissed, my heart thumping fast.

A faint, regular *swish, swish* and then a scrape. We looked at each other. I wanted to run for it, but I could see that Sally couldn't bear to go without knowing what it was. She crept towards the back of the house and very slowly and carefully peeped round the corner. Then she quickly dodged back, her hand clapped over her mouth. Well, of course I had to look, too, after that, and I was surprised, not at who it was but at what he was doing.

I knew him all right. All the kids knew him. We called him Mad Mason. He was the school caretaker who lived in the little gatehouse by the main road. He hated kids, and at the slightest excuse he'd shout like mad and chase us home, threatening to fetch the police.

It was what he was doing that amazed me, though when you think about it, he *was* only doing his job. He'd got a heavy spade and he was shovelling rubbish into a wheelbarrow beside an old stone-carved terrace that ran along the back of the house. As I watched he dumped his spade down, and climbed the crumbling stone steps that led up to the terrace. He went to a metal bucket, squeezed out a cloth and started trying to wipe off some of the rude words that had been painted on to the wall. But that house was so huge and so bashed up and covered with mess that he looked crazy. It was like somebody trying to sweep up the ocean, or snip down a forest with a pair of scissors.

"Stupid old git." Sally snorted.

I could see that she was about to burst out giggling. I shook my head at her. "Shut up!" I hissed.

We had to go. We had to get out of there fast, before she exploded. So we ran back the way we'd come, round the side of the house and past the front steps.

It was when we were back among the thickest laurels that I turned around for one last look. What I saw made my knees turn to jelly. I don't think I could have moved any further if Sally hadn't pulled me along. Then once I got going I went like the wind. What I'd seen up there in the top turret window was ... a face. A face that looked just as lost and sad as the whole house. But whoever it was had seen me, because they'd raised their hand and waved.

The Blues

....

We didn't stop running till we got home.
I dumped my schoolbag in our house and
yelled to my mother that I was going round
to Sally's.

"What?" she said puzzled. "Don't you
want a drink? Chocolate biscuit? Telly
programme?"

"Haven't time," I told her.

We sat on the wall in Sally's front garden and
couldn't stop talking.

"Whose house is it?"

"Who's smashed it up?"

"What's Mad Mason doing there?"

"There was someone up in the attic,
watching us!"

"No," said Sally. "I never saw anyone."

"Oh, yes there was," I told her. "A kid, I

think. Is it trespassing ... going in there?"

We hadn't any answers, but we couldn't ask our parents. That was one thing we both agreed on. If they had the faintest idea of what we'd been up to, that would be the end of it.

"We'll go back tomorrow," said Sally. "We'll go every day, but we musn't stay for long. Then they won't be suspicious."

I found it hard to get to sleep that night. When I did eventually manage it I kept dreaming about that face looking down at me from the turret window. I was sure that it was a boy, though he'd got rather long, wild curly hair and in my dream I could hear this throbbing, howling, sad kind of tune.

I was up and dressed early next morning; my mother couldn't believe it. I realized I'd better slow down a bit or I'd give the game away. Just as I was leaving for school, I slipped my mouth organ into my bag.

I don't really know what made me do it.

I never took my mouth organ to school.
I had to take my recorder every Friday for
recorder practice, but my mouth organ was
something I just mucked about with by
myself at home. I'd got a book called *Teach
Yourself Harmonica*. It was hard work, what
with all the sucking and blowing that you had
to do. I'd almost lost patience with it, but
then I'd seen this old black man on the telly.
He was playing a wailing tune on his
harmonica, and he played it so beautifully
that it made you want to cry. Then the man
talked in a deep gravelly voice about his
music. He called it the blues. Listening to him
had got me working away at my harmonica
again. That old man's music was just what
our lonely old house needed. It was the music
I'd heard in my dream. I wanted to sit there
on those beautiful, scruffy, bashed-up front
steps and play the blues.

We really wanted to go back to the house that
very morning, but we decided that it was too

risky. The fields and grounds were full of big kids and teachers all rushing past the wilderness towards the Comp.

"We'd be late," said Sally. "We'd spoil it all."

I had to agree. "I suppose so."

"Best if we wait till home time," she said. Then she got all bossy. "Make sure you get out quick! I'm not going to wait around for you!"

"Don't worry," I said. "I will."

The Holly and the Ivy

We were both out of school as fast as rabbits; no lurking in the cloakrooms that day. We waited casually by the laurel bushes until nobody else was in sight, then we plunged into the jungle. It was easier going, because we could follow the paths we'd made the day before.

"Look out for Mad Mason," Sally hissed.

We crept around the side of the house, listening carefully all the time. I kept glancing up at the turret window, but I couldn't see anything ... or anyone. Close to a smaller boarded-up side door, Sally found a pile of rubbish. She started scrabbling around in it. "Look !" she shouted triumphantly. "Cups, plates. They've got flowers and gold bits on."

"Yes," I said doubtfully. I could see that she'd found tiny pieces of china, but it was all hopelessly smashed.

"I might find all the bits," she said. "I might be able to stick them together."

I thought *she* was mad. Who'd want it anyway, a cracked, glued-together plate? I left her to it, and went cautiously round to the back of the house where we'd seen Mad Mason. He didn't seem to be there, but I saw his bucket and the heavy spade standing on the terrace where he'd been last time. I climbed up the wobbly stone steps and went to see what he'd been doing.

There were three dark, dusty windows set into the wall of the house, and between each window was a wonderful carving. The best one was of a dog dancing on its hind legs as though it were begging. It was so good, you could see the way the dog's ears were pricked. It even had all the tiny details right, whiskers and a tail that almost twitched with life. Underneath was a great ugly red circle of sprayed-on paint, with nonsense letters daubed in the middle. The top of the circle

cut right across the neat little carved feet of
the prancing dog.

I got out my mouth organ and put it to my
lips. I knew that it was a stupid thing to do,
but I just couldn't help it. I couldn't play the
blues, I wasn't good enough for that yet, but I
could play something for that little prancing
dog. It was the only tune that I knew well.

> *When the saints*
> *Go marching in*
> *Now when the saints go*
>   *marching in.*

It's a tune that my mother loves and
whenever I play it at home she starts jigging
around and singing. She says her gran used
to sing it to her when she was a little girl.
There at the wrecked house it came out all
loud and jolly, nothing like the blues I'd
wanted to play. I knew that it was going to
cause trouble, but I still couldn't stop myself
from doing it. The really weird thing was that

while I was playing, I could hear a different tune, that seemed to be floating in the air all around me. I stopped so that I could hear better, and just for a moment I did hear it, but the sound of it faded away quickly. Then, of course, round the corner came Sally, a piece of china in each hand. She was furious.

"What the heck? What the heck do you think you're playing at?" she shouted. "Do you want to tell all the world that we're here?"

"Sorry," I said. "I really wanted to play the blues!"

She looked at me as though I was completely barmy. I suppose I'm lucky that she didn't hit me.

"What?" she bellowed. "Play the what? Doesn't matter what the heck you play! Might as well ring a bell! Tell all the world we're here! You stupid idiot!"

And then, before she could say anything else, there came the sound of scuffling feet and footsteps. I was sure I saw the bushes shaking as though somebody was pushing them aside.

"Mad Mason," said Sally. "See! See what you've done! Come on! Got to go!"

We ran back down the side of the house, heading home the way we'd come, but I did glance back, and I saw who it was that had heard my tune. It wasn't old Mad Mason, as we'd feared, it was Gary Fox and his dopey mate Colin and the rest of the gang. They came sneaking out of the bushes from the other side.

Once I'd got home and calmed down a bit, it began to dawn on me what it all meant. Those nonsense words in red paint were Gs and Fs and Cs. Initials and signs made by the Fox Gang. I didn't have much doubt who it was that had been smashing the old place up and daubing their marks all over it.

Sally was so annoyed with me that night that we didn't do any talking at all. It was only much later when I was in bed that I remembered again the strange thing that had happened. When I'd played my mouth organ, someone else had played a different tune. I was quite sure that it had really happened, because I'd recognized the tune.

> *The Holly and the Ivy*
> *When they are both full grown*
> *Of all the trees that are in the wood*
> *The holly bears the crown.*

But whoever it was trying to jam along with me hadn't played a mouth organ. They'd been playing on something that sounded like one of our squeaky old school recorders.

Mad Mason

We walked to school in silence next morning. I tried to say that I was sorry, but Sally was still angry with me and she wouldn't even look at me. I spent most of the day thinking about the house and the crazy caretaker, especially when I was supposed to be doing maths. Mr Giles, who's usually quite a laugh, ended up snapping his fingers crossly in front of my face.

When I got out of school I saw that Sally was waiting for me as usual by the main gates. I walked up to her, gritting my teeth, ready for the telling off that I was going to get.

"Have you got that blooming mouth organ?" she asked.

I shook my head.

"Right then, come on, and if you make a

sound I'll ... I'll ... set Gary Fox on you!"

She couldn't help but smile a bit when she said it.

"Ha!" I said. "I'd like to see you. You'd be too scared yourself."

"I mean it," she said, all fierce again. "You make a sound and you'll regret it."

I followed her quite happily then. Sally was back to her usual self.

We pushed through the jungle and again we crept around until we were sure that nobody else was there. We went to the terrace at the back. It was strewn with bricks and slates and piled-up wood, but there, standing on the windowsill, was a bucket of soapy water, a knife and some screwed-up sandpaper. Mad Mason had been working away at his impossible task again.

"I can't understand what he's up to," said Sally, clomping over the rubbish. "He couldn't possibly make it nice again. Not by himself!"

"No," I agreed, sitting down on the terrace steps. "He'd need hundreds of cleaners. A whole army of them."

"He'd need carpenters too," said Sally. "And builders and decorators. He'd need glaziers for the smashed windows."

We both sighed. It was all so hopeless.

Sally went and fished around in the bucket. "This water's warm," she said. "He must have just gone."

She squeezed out the cloth, and started to scrub at a huge round blot of thick blue paint that was daubed on the sandy stonework between two windows. She shook her head and dropped the cloth. "Doesn't even come off. You wash at it for ever and can't get it off."

I picked up the sandpaper and clambered over the bricks and wood. I started to scratch away at the paint on the dog's feet. It was terrible work and it hurt my fingers, but at last I began to wear away a bit of the thick-set paint.

"This does it," I said. "If you work like crazy."

Sally picked up the old knife. "I'll try this," she said.

We worked so hard that we forgot the time. We seemed to forget about everything. Nothing mattered but shifting that great blot of paint. We'd just about got rid of the marks on one of the dog's little paws when we suddenly heard this awful grumpy voice behind us.

"Oh yes! Oh yes! I know you! I know what you're up to! I'll have the police on ... you!"

I dropped the sandpaper and my knees turned to jelly. Of course, it was Mad Mason and we hadn't even heard him coming. He charged round the corner of the house, growling threats and insults but as he got closer the grumpiness in his voice seemed to fade.

I wanted to run, and I would have done, but I've got to hand it to Sally. She just

turned around and gave him one of her really superior disgusted looks. Oh boy, it was such a look, it even frightened me, and then she calmly carried on scraping away at the wall.

I stared at Mad Mason for a moment or two, waiting for him to start shouting again, but he didn't. He just looked at us with his mouth open. I decided that the best thing to do was copy Sally, so I picked up the sandpaper, though my hands were shaking dreadfully.

"Just cleaning up," I said, my voice gone all squeaky. I forced my mouth into a smile and started trying to shift the paint again.

Mad Mason stood there shaking his head and watching us for ages, his hands just hanging at his sides. He didn't seem to know what to say.

When at last we'd removed the final lumps of blue paint from one paw, Sally looked down at her watch and gasped. "Oh damn!" she said. "We're late... Forgot the time."

"Got to go now," I said, putting the

sandpaper carefully back down beside the bucket.

He opened his mouth, then shut it again. A funny growly sound came from his throat.

"Is it all right if we come again?" Sally asked, all business-like about it.

Mad Mason just looked at her. "Cleaning it up," he muttered. "Not putting it on."

"That's right," said Sally. "Can we do some more?"

He still didn't answer, but he *did* nod his head.

Then we went.

Kind of ...
Got Permission

We made up a story about a lost dog and said we'd been talking to the caretaker about it. Our mothers seemed to believe us, and as Sally said, it wasn't all lies. We'd certainly been talking to the caretaker, and there had been a dog involved.

When we went to the house the next day we found a bucket of hot water, a cloth, fresh sandpaper and two blunt old knives. There was no sign of Mad Mason.

"See," said Sally. "It's all right. We've kind of ... got permission."

"OK," I said, still feeling a bit unsure. "I'm going to finish the dog."

"I like this one with the roses," said Sally. "But we'd better do one thing at a time. We won't go until we've got the little dog clean."

We had to stand on top of the rubble to

reach the dog carving. Beside us was a tall window. We could see into an empty, dust-filled room, with great raggy bits of plaster hanging off the ceiling. At least the window wasn't smashed like some of them. I looked down and tapped my toe on a line of stonework. I could see a neat edge and then what looked like carved stripes, but the great heap of rubble that we were standing on covered it up.

"There's a pattern down there," I said. "Could be another picture."

"I said one thing at a time," Sally told me sharply. "It'd take us ages to shift all that stuff."

It was terribly hard work again. The paint seemed to have seeped right into the carefully carved little claws and feet of the dog. At one point I threw down my knife and stood back.

"We'll never get it clean," I said.

"No ... not if you mess about like that," said Sally.

I was just thinking of a clever reply when I

glanced up towards the high turret window on the far side of the house. I saw him again, the boy with the wild curly hair. He was leaning out of the window, smiling and making a thumbs-up sign.

"Hey," I said to Sally. "He's there again. That lad that I told you about. Come and look at him!" I grabbed her and pulled her back with me, among the overgrown bushes, so that she could see him too.

"Where?" she said. "Where? I can't see anything."

And she was right. When I looked up at that top window again he'd gone.

"He's hiding," I said. "Teasing us." I put my hand up to my mouth and shouted, "Hoy! What you doing there?"

There was no answer and Sally suddenly looked a bit worried. "Not Gary Fox, is it?"

"No," I said. "Definitely not him, or any of his gang. He looked OK, sort of friendly. Like he was egging us on."

"Couldn't be *his* house, could it?" said

Sally. "Come on, let's get going or we'll never get it done."

We set about the little dog with a bit more energy, but while we worked I thought I heard that faint squeaky recorder music again. Whenever I stopped scraping to listen properly, it seemed to vanish, and whenever I started work again I was sure that I could hear it. We'd almost got the little dog free of paint when Mad Mason arrived. He stood and watched us in silence for a bit, then he suddenly made us jump.

"What you wanna do this for?" he growled.

"I like him," I said, and I patted the little dog's stone head.

"Well, *you* were cleaning it," said Sally, dead confident. "Why were *you* cleaning it up?"

"Ah," he said. "I got my reasons see ... good reasons."

"Whose house is it anyway?" said Sally.

"Hard to say." Mad Mason still sounded

gruff and grumpy. "Belongs to the Education Department, I suppose. It's Council land. Rich family of steel owners had it built – Holton Grange Manor."

"Holton Grange Manor?" said Sally. "That's what they call the Comp."

"Ha ... that place!" Mad Mason's voice was full of scorn. "They built it on Holton Grange land and named it after this house. Fancy naming that blooming great lump of modern concrete after this fine old place."

Mad Mason's face turned angry and red at the thought of it and I began to understand his grumpiness a bit.

"Why has it been left like this?" I asked.

He shrugged his shoulders. "They're barmy," he said. "Too expensive to keep up, that's what they said, but that was years ago. Just forgotten about it and left it to fall into ruin."

Then suddenly his voice went all soft. "But it's a beautiful old place right enough, and

my grandfather was the stonemason. He
made all these carvings."

Tilly's Tunes

....

I stared open-mouthed for a moment while it sank in. "You mean ... it was your grandfather who carved the little dog?"

"Oh, yes. That was Tilly, my father's dog. Smashing little terrier."

"Did you know her?" Sally demanded.

"Know her? You silly lass!" Mad Mason laughed disgustingly, so that we could see all his missing teeth. "I'm not as old as that. What do you think I am," he snapped, "a hundred?"

Sally shrugged her shoulders and frowned. "How was I to know?"

They glared at each other for a moment. Then suddenly Mad Mason seemed to soften a bit.

"My father was just a young nipper when this house was built. He used to play here while my grandfather was making all these patterns in the stone. He loved this place, did my dad."

"So," I said, trying to work it all out. "Your grandfather made the carvings, and your dad was a young lad playing here?"

"That's right. Look there, beneath Tilly's feet! Can you see the chisel marks, in the shape of a tiny rose?"

"Yes," Sally almost shrieked with excitement. "Yes ... a tiny rose!"

"That's Grandfather Mason's signature," said Mad Mason proudly. "You'll find that tiny rose on every bit of carving he did. My father, George, and his little dog, Tilly, had a smashing time here while grandfather was working. When he was older he told me all about it. Always on about Holton Grange Manor was George. He's been dead a good while now, and Tilly long gone, of course."

We watched, surprised, as Mad Mason went and gently patted the back of the prancing stone terrier. "You've done a grand job," he told us. "You've cleaned her up good and proper." Then suddenly his voice turned nasty again. "And if ever I get my hands on those blasted, trespassing—"

"Are we trespassing?" Sally asked. "Are we allowed here?"

Mad Mason frowned then and looked a bit puzzled. "Well now," he said at last. "I'm caretaker in charge of the whole site. You're all right if I give permission."

We waited then, while he stood there with his arms folded, looking important.

At last I sighed and asked him. "Well ... do you give permission?"

He thought again for a moment. "I suppose so," he said.

We started going every day, and we spent longer and longer there, working away at the house. We even decided that we'd have to tell our mothers.

"We've got permission," we insisted.

They looked at each other in that

suspicious, worried way that mothers have.

"Ooh ... don't like the sound of that."

"I do remember the old house. Thought it had been pulled down years ago."

"Might be dangerous ... don't you think?"

Both our mothers came scrambling through the bushes after us to see what it was all about. They talked to Mad Mason, who suddenly became terribly polite. He told us to call him Bill and brought out a heavy old key ring from his pocket. "Want to have a look inside?" he asked.

He led us through huge, cold rooms, coated in dust and cobwebs. We looked up at wonderful plaster patterns on damp ceilings, ancient musty-smelling panelling on the walls. Our mothers followed Bill with amazement.

"The space," they said.

"The craftsmanship!"

"The waste ... the terrible waste!"

"Too expensive to maintain," Bill told them. "That's what they said. Shan't take you

upstairs ... not safe, those stairs."

"Oh, but I've seen someone up there in the turret," I said. "A boy with long curly hair. He plays the recorder."

He stared at me for a moment as though he almost believed me, but then he suddenly shook his head. "No," he said. "Can't have been. Can't see how those damned hooligans could have got up there. Stairs all rotten in the turret. They'd do themselves damage... Serve them right too!"

Our mothers went away talking about campaigns to save the house, and writing letters to the paper, letters to the Council. They didn't actually get round to doing it. Still, all we cared about was that they didn't seem to mind us going to the house any more.

Making Their Marks

We cleaned the rose carving and another
with funny long flowers. We'd started work
on a pattern of ivy leaves and holly covered
with tiny stone berries when the summer
holidays began. We hunted for the tiny
chiselled rose signature each time we started
a new job.

Bill told us so much about his father and
grandfather that I almost felt I knew them
myself. When Abraham Troutsdale, the rich
steel owner, had built his fine new home, he'd
wanted it covered with beautiful carvings.

"That fish above the big front door,"
Bill said, "was for his name, Troutsdale, and
the sword for the steel they made at his
works."

"How did little dog Tilly get here?" Sally
asked.

"Well, now. Once he'd got his fish and sword, old man Troutsdale didn't care what else went on to his house, so long as the work was good. He allowed my grandfather to carve whatever patterns he liked."

A weird, creepy feeling came over me as he spoke, for suddenly I knew what he was going to tell us next.

"Your grandfather carved the little dog to please your dad," I said.

"That's right. How did you know?"

I shrugged my shoulders and shook my head.

Bill pointed to the rose pattern. "Now this one he carved to please my grandmother. Roses were her favourite flower."

"What about these?" Sally asked. "The holly and the ivy?"

I knew the answer again, and a little shiver of excitement ran through me.

"Songs!" I shouted. "This one's a carol, 'The Holly and the Ivy', and this one's 'Lavender's Blue'. Look at the long stalks of

lavender, and the neat flowers."

"Oh," said Sally. "Were they *his* favourite flowers?"

"No, they weren't!" I yelled. "They were the tunes that young George played on his recorder, over and over again."

Old Bill stared at me then and scratched his head. "I think it was a penny whistle," he muttered. He looked almost offended that I should have got it right. But I had a clear picture in my mind of a tough young lad with wild curly hair running about the building with Tilly, playing the only two tunes that he knew on a home-made pipe, while Grandfather Mason worked away on the stone carvings.

"Tunes for Tilly," I said.

"You're going daft," said Sally.

"Your grandfather put his marks all over the house," I said. "Even though it really belonged to Abraham Troutsdale."

Bill suddenly looked angry. "Put his marks all over the house?" he said. "It was his job!"

"Yes," I said, a bit shaky. "Didn't mean anything bad."

Bill thought for a moment. He seemed quite upset by what I'd said. "Dammit, you're right," he said. "Marks? Their own marks? Is that what these blasted vandals think they're doing?"

I hadn't thought about it like that. The mess around the house was horrible, and most of the graffiti was horrible too, but there were just one or two bits where you could see the carefully painted shape of an animal, or the lines of a pattern.

"Well, putting their marks or not, they'd better not let me catch them at it," Bill growled.

Sally had said that I was going daft, and at times I wondered if she was right. The house seemed to be taking me over. Sometimes we tried to do something different, like go swimming or boating on the lake, but we'd get bored and end up back at old Holton

Grange. The more we worked and scrubbed at the house, the more we could see it as it had once been, splendid and clean and beautiful.

Sometimes while we worked we heard sniggering and rustling in the bushes behind us, but if we stopped and looked around there'd be nothing to see. We knew who it was, of course. When we passed Gary Fox's gang hanging out in the woods, bored with smoking, they'd entertain themselves by making funny comments about us.

"Where's your bucket and mop then?" "Where's your apron Danny Boy? Going to help Mad Mason?" "Hey ... who could have smashed up the old dump?"

I hated it, and I hated them, but I gritted my teeth and ignored them. Gary Fox was quite small really, and he was good at looking innocent when he needed to, but he watched us coming and going like a weasel. I suppose in a way we were spoiling their holiday fun.

While we were at the house with old Bill they couldn't start messing it up again, or at least they couldn't do it without us seeing them.

It was the middle of the summer holidays when the dreadful thing happened. Sally and I spent the whole morning scraping away a huge blot of red and blue spray paint from the lavender carving. It was hot and we knew that we were being watched. There were owl hoots and giggling and rustling in the bushes. We went home for our lunch and it was when we went back to the house in the afternoon that we saw it.

The Attack

....

Sally saw it first, but it was only because she
was walking ahead of me. Really, you
couldn't miss it.

I'm used to hearing awful language from
Sally, but you *should* have heard the swear
words that came from her that day! I rushed
up the old terrace steps to see what was
wrong. I just couldn't believe it. It took my
breath away. Little dog Tilly was covered in
hideous red paint.

We stared at it in disbelief, but almost at
once we heard sniggering behind us. I
turned around. At first I could see nothing,
but the branches and bushes all about us
were shaking. Then I saw Gary Fox grinning
at me from behind a thick-leafed laurel bush.
His face was pink with excitement.

"Yeah, get 'em!" he yelled.

Then suddenly there were boys coming from every bush, their arms full of bricks and stones. They hurled their missiles at the house, the windows and us.

There was a crash and a crack, and the window beside Tilly was smashed. Something snapped in me. I went crazy. I could see that for once Sally was scared, and that made me even more furious. I picked up the heavy spade that Bill had left propped against the top of the stone terrace.

"I'm gonna get you!" I shouted. "I'm gonna get you! All of you!" I screamed and bellowed, lurching towards them, waving the spade. They stopped throwing stones and stared in horror.

Somehow, what with the speed and the madness that I felt, I must have kicked out one of the big loose stones at the top of the terrace steps because the ground seemed to give way beneath me. Still clutching the spade, I tumbled head first down the steps, down towards Gary Fox.

There was a nasty crack as I landed at Gary Fox's feet. I vaguely supposed that it was the sound of the spade clattering against the stonework. Sally screamed as I fell, and for a moment I couldn't seem to catch my breath. It was only when I tried to get up that I knew something was terribly wrong.

"No, don't touch him," a voice close by shouted. "Look at his leg!"

I forced myself to sit up and look. My leg wasn't bleeding, but there was certainly something about it that looked odd. It was almost as though it was bent the wrong way round and when I tried to shift it ... it hurt. It really hurt like hell!

"Don't move. Don't even try to move," someone said. I looked up into the face of Gary Fox and suddenly I felt as though I was going to be sick. Gary's face had gone deadly white and he pushed me back.

"Don't move," he said. "Gotta broken leg."

I looked up at him, and even though my stomach was heaving, I was amazed. It *was*

Gary Fox who'd been talking to me. He looked scared, but what was even stranger was that he was actually trying to help. That shocked me as much as what had happened to my leg. As I stared up at him black dots began to speckle his face and the sickness faded.

"Out the way – let me see!" I heard Bill's voice shouting, then all at once the black dots joined up, and the whole world went black. I couldn't see Gary Fox's face any more.

The Boy
With the Pipe

I heard the music even before I opened my eyes. The pain had vanished and I was warm and comfortable. There was a scraping sound in the distance and then a regular *tap, tap, tap*ping. The squeaky pipe music started again, close by. Closer than I had ever heard it before.

> *Lavender's blue, dilly dilly,*
> *Lavender's green,*
> *When I am king, dilly dilly,*
> *You shall be queen.*

Though my eyes were closed I could feel the sun on my eyelids. Suddenly I was filled with an unbearable excitement. Was it possible? Was he really there beside me this time? The boy with the penny whistle! I'd wanted him to

come down from the turret and speak to me.
I'd wanted it more than anything. Could
something as wonderful as this really happen?
Soft whiskers brushed my cheek and I could
hear snuffly breathing close beside me.
Happiness spread through my body as
something warm and wet touched the side of
my face. I opened my eyes slowly, fearful that
I'd be disappointed, but there they were, both
of them, sitting beside me – the curly haired
boy and his dog.

Tilly woofed joyfully as I sat up.

"Are you George?" I said to the boy.

"'Course I am," he grinned. He didn't
seem at all surprised to see me.

We were both sitting on the top step of the
terrace. He held his pipe in his hands and
when I looked at it properly I saw that it was
straight and looked home made. Bill had
called it a penny whistle.

George winked at me as though he saw me
there every day.

"Here," he said. "Have a look. I've nearly

finished another one."

I took the pipe, and carefully felt the smooth sanded wood. "I can touch it," I said.

He laughed again as though he thought I was funny. I turned around, stretching out my hand to little Tilly. It was wonderful to feel her warm bony head, the smooth hairs on the top, and the softness of her floppy ears.

I saw the pipe that George had almost completed in his lap. He set about finishing it, cutting out the last hole with a small, sharp knife.

While he worked I stared about me, knowing just what I'd see, but wanting to remember every little detail.

The house was newly built, its sandstone gleaming golden and yellow in the sunlight. The distant tapping and scraping was the sound of Grandfather Mason working away with his hammer and chisel, somewhere round the side of the house. Above me the carving of Tilly was fresh and sharp, as if it had just been finished that very day.

But then I caught my breath and stood up for a better look. There was the lovely stone oval with the roses in it, but where was "The Holly and the Ivy" and where was "Lavender's Blue"? There were two blank plaques of stone where the carvings should be, and no sign at all of any patterns beneath Tilly.

"What's up?" said George.

"There should be patterns here," I told him. "Patterns for your tunes."

"Don't know what you mean," he said.

He put down his knife and held up the new pipe for me to admire. "Finished that anyway. Good little whistle, this."

He put the new pipe to his lips and tooted down it. "Sounds all right," he said, satisfied.

"Play 'The Holly and the Ivy'," I said. "You're good at that."

"I like your tune," he said. "That jolly marching tune."

I couldn't understand what he meant for a

moment, then it dawned on me. " 'When the Saints Go Marching In'," I said.

"I think that's it," he nodded. "Play it for me."

He nodded at the pipe that I still held. I looked at it doubtfully. It had the same number of holes as my recorder. "Don't know if I can."

But Tilly nuzzled my hand, giving me encouragement and I put the pipe to my lips. The tune came easily and George copied me. He was slow at first, but he did it over and over again until he knew the notes. At last we played together.

"Has it got words?" he asked.

"Yes," I said. "But I can't start singing here. My mother would, but I can't."

"You can't sing?" said George, clearly surprised.

"I'd feel daft!"

"Go on," he begged. "I can't learn the words if you don't sing them."

He seemed so keen that in the end I gave

in. George played the tune and I sang the words.

> *When the saints*
> *Go marching in*
> *Now – when the saints go marching in.*
> *I want to be in that number.*
> *When the saints go marching in.*

As I sang the words I felt wonderfully happy. Tilly got up on her hind legs and pranced joyfully round in a circle in time to our tune. I could see her clearly, her pink tongue, the shiny black and white hairs in her smooth coat, the lovely floppy way her ears bent forward. Beyond her was the stretch of flat rolled earth that would one day be a neat lawn and then eventually a jungle. There were newly planted saplings, oaks and yews that would grow taller than the house itself.

But gradually the scene became speckled with those tiny black dots. Suddenly they swam out to meet each other and once again everything went black.

Desperate Dan

....

Then I was back again with that awful pain. I could hear myself groaning.

"Breathe in, love. It'll help... Honestly it will."

It was my mother's voice and she was close there beside me. There was a funny smell and a strange black mask in front of my face. I felt as though I was floating on a bed that joggled and joggled about.

"Where am I?"

"It's all right, love," came my mother's voice. Soft fingers stroked my cheek. "You're in an ambulance. We're on our way to hospital. They're going to put everything right. You've banged your head and you've got a broken leg."

"Oh, no," I groaned again.

"Here ... breathe into this mask." A man's

deep voice spoke firmly. "Bit of gas and air. You'll feel much better then."

So though it smelt weird, I did breathe deeply, and they were right. The pain faded and I thought that I floated off on a cloud into a beautiful blue sky.

There were bumps and thumps and I knew that I was lifted up and then down and wheeled along on a trolley, but whenever my leg hurt badly I gulped in some of that marvellous gas and air stuff and went floating off again.

There were doctors and nurses asking me all sorts of questions, till I got fed up with it, but my mother was there, and she did a lot of answering too. Somebody stuck a needle in the top of my leg, which I really thought was a bit much on top of everything else. I shouted, "Ouch!"

"That'll make you feel much better," they told me. And they were right, it did.

They X-rayed my leg, then two cheerful nurses plastered it from top to bottom.

"Dear me, what's the other fellow look like?" they said.

"Wasn't a fellow," I told them. "It was old stone steps."

"Well, I hope they're still standing."

"Probably not," I muttered. "Whole house is a ruin."

"Who did you think you were?" they said. "Desperate Dan?"

I was wheeled up to the ward and my father came rushing in through the swing doors, looking white faced and worried.

"Just got the message from Sally," he said. "Whatever have you been doing, son?"

They both sat down either side of my bed. At last I felt really safe and looked after, tucked up in that hospital bed, with the rustling of nurses' uniforms and kind voices all around me. I suddenly felt exhausted.

"Want to go to sleep," I muttered.

"Best thing," said my mother. "You shut your eyes."

* * *

When I woke up it was morning. There were bright lights and the clattering of pots, and my leg hurt badly.

"How do you feel?" my mother asked.

"Terrible," I said. "Have you been here all night?"

"No," she said. "I've been home and come back again. Your dad's gone off to work."

"Would you like porridge, dear?" someone asked me.

"No," I said. "I'd be sick. Can't eat when my leg hurts like this."

"Oh, dear," my mother said.

I knew that I was being a little bit rude, but I didn't care.

"Don't worry," said the nurse. "You're due for another injection, I think."

I didn't argue. I knew by now that a small sharp pain was well worth it. I soon drifted off to sleep again.

I slept and slept, drifting in and out of strange dreams. Sometimes I thought I was back at the house with Tilly and George.

At last I opened my eyes to the bright lights of the hospital ward, and I couldn't believe what I saw. I shut my eyes again quickly, thinking that I must be still dreaming. But when I tried again they were still there, standing at the bottom of my bed, the strangest mixture of people I could possibly imagine.

Strange Visitors

There was Sally looking worried and Bill looking very clean and smart, wearing a suit. Next to him was Colin, all big and awkward with a box of chocolates in his hands. Then, behind Colin, was Gary Fox, shyly standing back a little.

My mouth must have dropped open with surprise. I couldn't think what on earth to say. I looked from one to the other still unbelieving.

My surprised look seemed to shake Sally out of her fright. She grinned.

"You should see your face," she said.

Then suddenly we were laughing. Even Gary Fox was giggling in an embarrassed way.

"What's all this row about?" said a passing nurse. That seemed to make us laugh all the more.

When we eventually managed to calm down we started talking.

"I don't even know what really happened," I said.

They all tried to tell me at once.

"You fell," said Sally. "Right from the top of the stairs to the bottom."

"It was this young varmint that knew what to do," said Bill, and he touched Gary Fox's arm. "He thought your leg was broken and knew that we shouldn't try to move you."

Gary Fox looked even more embarrassed. "Had a broken leg myself, when I were only five years old," he muttered. "Horrible, i'n't it?"

Suddenly I realized that my leg was only aching a bit. The really terrible pain had gone.

"Not so bad now," I said.

"Sally ran to fetch your mother," said Bill. "And this lad," and he put his arm round Colin's huge shoulders. "This lad ... ran down to my cottage and telephoned for an ambulance."

Colin grinned hugely. "Dialled 999," he said. "Always wanted to do that!"

"I've got to say it," said Bill. "He showed a lot of sense. He stood by the gate till the ambulance came and waved them in. He brought them up the old carriage drive and showed them where you were."

"The police have been," said Sally importantly. "They've been asking questions about the accident and about the house."

"The house," I said. "What about the house?"

"Got the men from the Council coming," said Bill. "Coming to look at it, see if it's dangerous." He shrugged his shoulders.

"Well, it is dangerous, isn't it?" said Sally.

"What will they do?" I asked.

Bill looked miserable. "Pull it down, I suppose."

"Was there trouble with the police?" I asked. Gary Fox went very red and stared at the floor.

"There could have been," said Bill. "I *could*

have reported all this lot for trespassing and vandalism." He waved accusingly at the two boys. Colin smiled stupidly. "But I didn't. They could have run off when you fell. Could have got clean away... But they stayed and helped. They've promised me that there'll be no more trouble. So, well, we'll see."

I nodded. I couldn't help feeling that they'd got off lightly, but then I remembered that I *had* gone after them with a big spade.

There was a rattling of plates and cutlery. One of the nurses wheeled a trolley up to us. "Tea-time," she said. "Fish and chips suit you?"

"Oh, yes please," I said. "I'm starving."

I spent a few days in hospital fussed over by my mother. Visitors came and went with lots of news. First I heard that the men from the Council had looked over Holton Grange Manor and shaken their heads. But then they'd called in historians and architects to have a look, and they'd said that such an interesting historical building really should be saved.

Sally turned up at the hospital all rushed and excited. "Can't stay long," she said. "Going knocking on doors, with my dad. Got a petition organized!"

"What do you mean?" I asked.

"Petition to save the house," she said. "Everyone's signing it. All the school! Gary Fox's taking it round the Comp. He's making all the kids sign – teachers too."

I was speechless!

The New Annexe

The day I came home from hospital I was desperate to go over to Holton Grange, but it was impossible. My leg was encased from toes to thigh in a heavy white plaster. It was hard enough to walk around my house on crutches, let alone go struggling through a jungle of overgrown bushes.

I wanted to help with the petition, but I had to sit uselessly in my front room, watching Sally rush about doing it. My dad suggested that perhaps I could do some letter writing. I turned up my nose at first, but I was so bored that I thought I might as well have a go. I wrote a letter to the local paper, telling them all about the house and about Bill's grandfather and his wonderful carvings.

A few days later Sally came knocking at our door first thing in the morning, before we'd even got up. She was red in the face and waving the paper wildly about.

"You've got in the paper!" she yelled. "Star letter of the week! You win ten pounds!"

"What?" I cried.

My hands wouldn't stop shaking as I read it. They'd put a big heading above it:

YOUNG ACCIDENT VICTIM FIGHTS TO SAVE GRANGE

There was no stopping me then. I wrote to the Council. I wrote to the Education Offices. I wrote to our Member of Parliament.

By the time the autumn term started, I was very bored and miserable again and almost glad to go back to school. I had to be taken there and back by taxi. My father grumbled like mad about the extra money it cost, but my mother said that Sally might as well go in the taxi with me as that wouldn't cost any more.

I had to be patient about the house and I had to be patient while my leg got better. It was very hard to be *so* patient. I got angry and rude and fed up.

Then one evening when Sally was watching telly round at our house, Bill came knocking on our door. His face was just one huge, great smile. He came and stood in front of our fireplace and grinned from ear to ear.

"Can't believe it," he said. "Just can't believe it."

"What is it?" we asked. But we all began to smile too.

"Gonna be all right," he said. "Gonna be saved!"

"How?" we cried. "How?"

"Too many children," he said.

We couldn't understand what he was on about. Then, as he explained it slowly to us, we began to see.

"Few years ago," said Bill, "they closed down some of the smaller schools. Dropping numbers, see! Sent all the kids to Holton

Comp. Now they've found the numbers are going up again. They've been thinking of building on new classrooms and offices."

"So ... they could use the old Manor House instead."

"That's it. They've told me for definite today. Gonna clean it and do it all up. It's your petitions and letters that have made them realize they've got a wonderful old building just waiting there. It's going to be the new comprehensive school annexe."

Sally and me went wild, cheering and yelling. If I could have, I'd have got up and danced around the room. When we'd calmed down again Bill told us cheerfully that he'd got the sack.

"Oh, no," my mother cried. "How terrible."

But Bill could do nothing but laugh and shake his head. "Too much for me," he said, "being in charge of the whole site. They say that I can stay in my cottage, and I've got a new job now. Caretaker of the new school annexe. Best job in the world for me."

Banishing the Blues

···

As the weather grew cold, workmen came
and set up barriers all around Holton
Grange. Sometimes we could hear the distant
whirr of sandblasting machines from our
school. At half term I had to go back to the
hospital. The huge, heavy plaster was
removed from my leg by two fierce and jolly
dragon nurses, who terrified me when they
came at me with little whirling saws.

"Watch it!" I shrieked.

"Oh, you're not scared of these, are you?"
They laughed.

One of them snatched up my hand and
touched my palm with the fearsome blade. I
gasped and waited for the blood to spurt, but
it never came. It tickled a bit, that's all.

"See," she said. "These saws don't cut
skin, only plaster. Now then, young man, you

have to have a smaller fibreglass plaster on for a few weeks. Do you want red or blue?"

"Blue," I said.

"Of course ... blue for a boy."

"No. Lavender's blue," I said.

"What a lovely lad," said the nurse, and she gave me the most revolting sloppy kiss.

I was completely out of plaster by Christmas, but it still took a long time to get used to walking properly again. My leg seemed to have gone all weak and wobbly, but before it was Eastertime, Sally and I were once more walking through the school grounds.

We often went to see Bill in his cottage by the school gates. Sometimes we tried to look through the barricades to see what they were doing to our old house. We got small glimpses of beautiful clean stonework, while our noses twitched at the strong smell of fresh paint, but we couldn't really see the place properly. Then at last the date was set for a grand re-opening. One week before the opening the barriers were taken down. As soon as we heard, Sally and I set off to have a look, and of course our mothers had to come too.

The workmen had left a lot of the old yew trees standing around the house, so that you couldn't see it from miles away, but as we got closer, we had to stop and stare. The turret rose gleaming with clean golden stonework from its setting of trees and bushes.

"A fairytale castle," said Sally.

I knew just what she meant. The high window sparkled in the bright sunlight, and I'm sure I saw a small figure up there, waving madly to me. Whether I really saw him or not, I knew he was there.

Bill was standing on the front steps talking to the headmistress, but as soon as he saw us he stopped and insisted on giving us a tour of the building.

He showed us the refurbished and decorated hallway. Then we were able to walk up the now-sturdy staircase and peep into classrooms, science labs, art rooms and offices.

"Could we go up to the turret?" I begged.

"'Course you can," he said. "You've got to see what they've done with the little room at the top."

We followed him up a firm, winding stair that smelt of fresh paint and new wood. Bill flung open the door and I peeped rather nervously into a small round room. All it contained was a keyboard, two guitars and a set of recorders.

"Music room," Bill told us. "They can make as much noise as they like up here. Won't bother a soul."

My eyes filled up with tears.

No, I thought. It won't bother him. It'll delight him.

"Oh, isn't it wonderful?" our mothers kept saying. "Oh, isn't this just what we hoped for!"

We all trooped back down into the hallway,

and past two huge blank boards that covered most of the long walls. "Now this," said Bill proudly, "is my idea. They're going to get the kids to paint whatever they like on these boards. I suggested it to the head – and do you know, she took notice of me."

"What a good idea," said my mother.

"Yes," Bill insisted. "I said to her, 'Let them put their marks on the place, then maybe they'll want to look after it.' It was something young Dan once said to me that made me think of it."

Sally and I grinned at each other.

When at last we'd finished our tour, Bill insisted that we follow him outside.

"I've something else to show you," he told us.

We walked down the side of the building and round to the terrace. I wanted to cry again with happiness when I saw what a lovely job they'd done on Tilly. Every trace of red paint had gone, and the carving was as fresh and sharp as the day she was made.

"Now look what they found," said Bill. He pointed to the carving beneath Tilly that used to be covered up with rubbish. We'd always wondered what the funny stripes could be. Now we knew. The stripes were the ends of rays that beamed out from a round sun.

Then beneath it was a line of small figures marching along, playing all sorts of musical instruments.

Sally grabbed my arm. "Another song," she said. "Your song."

Then suddenly I understood. " 'When the Saints Go Marching In'!" I yelled.

"If only my father could see it," said Bill. "Old George'd be that pleased."

"He *can* see it," I said. "I'm sure he can."

"Aye ... maybe he can," said Bill quietly.

Suddenly my mother started jigging about and singing the song. Sally clapped and snapped her fingers and tapped her feet. Even though it was very embarrassing to have your mother do that, for once I just stood there and grinned. I think I was the only one

who could hear a squeaky home-made pipe
playing the same tune.